THE LIFE OF
ANNE FRANK

By
Dr. Nicholas Saunders

School Specialty
Publishing

Anne Frank: *Born in 1929, Anneliese Marie, called Anne, Frank was a German-Jewish teenager who was forced to go into hiding during World War II. After the Nazis discovered their hiding place, Anne and her family were arrested and sent to a Nazi concentration camp. In March 1945, she died at the Bergen-Belsen camp, at the age of 15. While in hiding, she wrote a diary, which has become one of most widely read books in the world.*

Otto Frank: *After serving in the German army during World War I, Anne's father, Otto, worked in a bank. Following Hitler's rise to power in 1933, he started a new business in Amsterdam. The Frank family hid above the offices during the war. Modest, kind, and resourceful, Mr. Frank tutored Anne and her sister and calmed everyone's nerves during moments of crisis. He was the only member of the secret apartment to survive the war. Otto published Anne's diary in 1947.*

Margot Frank: *Three years older than Anne, Margot was considered more beautiful and intelligent than Anne. During the two years they were confined in the apartment, the two sisters became close friends. After the group was sent to the concentration camps, Anne and Margot managed to remain together almost until the end. Like Anne, Margot died of typhus at the Bergen-Belsen camp in March 1945.*

Edith Frank: *Born in 1900, Edith Hollander, Anne's mother, grew up in the town of Aachen and moved to Frankfurt after marrying Otto Frank in 1925. Edith was used to living in a big house with servants. She found life in the secret apartment very difficult—perhaps one reason she and Anne did not always get along well. Edith died of starvation at the Auschwitz camp in Janaury 1945, just days before the German guards fled the camp.*

Peter van Pels: *Peter was the son of Hermann van Pels, who went into business with Otto Frank in 1938. Peter's family fled from Germany the previous year and moved into the secret apartment a week after the Frank family. A simple but kind boy, Peter was sometimes teased by Anne. As time passed, Anne gradually became close to Peter, eventually falling in love with him. They were separated at the Auschwitz camp. Peter died a few months later during a forced march in freezing conditions.*

Miep Gies: *Miep worked for Otto Frank's Opekta company in Amsterdam. She helped the Frank and van Pels families hide during the war. Miep brought them food and news from the outside. She organized gifts and surprises on birthdays and festivals, and did what she could to make life better for the hidden families. It was Miep who found and hid Anne Frank's diary after the family's arrest. She later gave the diary to Otto after the war.*

School Specialty. Publishing

Copyright © ticktock Entertainment Ltd. 2006 First published in Great Britain in 2006 by ticktock Media Ltd., Unit 2, Orchard Business Centre, North Farm Road, Tunbridge Wells, Kent, TN2 3XF. This edition published in 2006 by School Specialty Publishing, a member of the School Specialty Family. Send all inquiries to School Specialty Publishing, 8720 Orion Place, Columbus, OH 43240.

Hardback ISBN 0-7696-4714-6   Paperback ISBN 0-7696-4695-6
1 2 3 4 5 6 7 8 9 10 TTM 10 09 08 07 06
Printed in China.

CONTENTS

In 1918, the world had been at war for over three years. Over 15 million soldiers and civilians had died. By the summer of 1918, the Allies, including France, the U.S., and Britain, had gained the upper hand and were defeating the Central Powers, which included Germany.

AAARGH! BOOM!

By November, the Germans had surrendered. At the Treaty of Versailles, the Allies forced Germany to pay them huge sums of money, called reparations. Germany also lost territory.

Germany must be punished for starting the war!

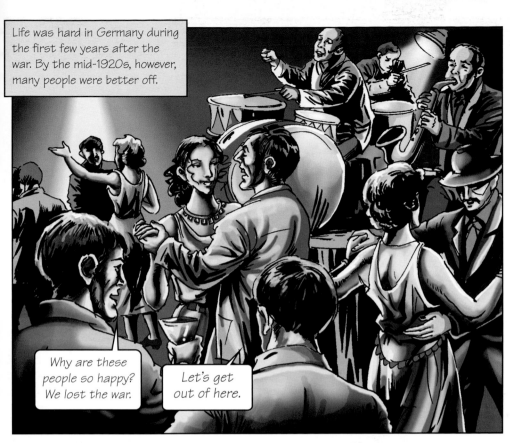

Life was hard in Germany during the first few years after the war. By the mid-1920s, however, many people were better off.

Why are these people so happy? We lost the war.

Let's get out of here.

We could have won. Now, look at Germany.

Our lousy politicians stabbed us in the back.

Many German ex-soldiers were still angry about losing the war. They blamed the new government for the Treaty of Versailles.

One of these bitter ex-soldiers, Adolf Hitler, led a new party, the National Socialists, or Nazis.

People are angry and afraid. I can use that to help us get into power.

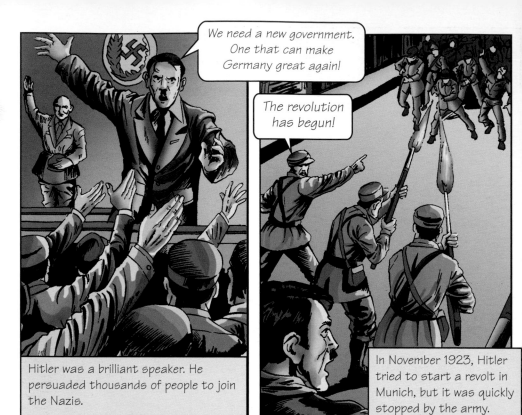

Hitler was a brilliant speaker. He persuaded thousands of people to join the Nazis.

In November 1923, Hitler tried to start a revolt in Munich, but it was quickly stopped by the army.

Hitler was sent to prison for 9 months. This gave him time to think about how to gain power. While he was in prison, he wrote a book about his plan, called *Mein Kampf* (*My Struggle*). At first, the Nazis weren't very popular. Then, in 1929, the German economy collapsed. Many workers lost their jobs and their savings.

More and more people hoped that Hitler would make Germany strong again. He blamed the Jews for all their problems, and many Germans believed him.

People will vote me into power.

The Jews are stealing your jobs and your money. It's time to fight back!

You're right! It's all their fault.

APPLAUSE

Hitler's private army, the "storm troopers," began to attack Jewish shops and buildings.

SMASH!

Go back to where you came from!

Take that, you dirty Jews!

This was the world that Anne Frank grew up in, where simply being Jewish could lead to attacks, imprisonments, and murder.

FAST FACT The Nazi swastika designed by Hitler was based on an ancient symbol that has been in use for over 3,000 years. It originally stood for life and goodness.

7

Anne Frank was born on June 12, 1929. She was the second daughter of Otto and Edith Frank, who were German Jews. The Franks lived in Frankfurt, Germany. Members of their family had lived there for 300 years.

Margot, meet your new sister, Anne!

Frankfurt

In 1929, there were about 30,000 Jews living in Frankfurt, for the most part a tolerant city.

FAST FACT Attacks on Jewish people had happened since the Middle Ages, but by the 20th century, Jews were able to live in peace in many parts of Europe. Jews had lived in Europe for over 2,000 years. By the time Hitler came to power in 1933, there were around nine million Jews living in Europe.

Like many Jews, Otto Frank had fought for the German army during World War I.

Otto's brother, Robert   Otto

After the war, Otto worked at his father's bank. At this time, he met Anne's mother Edith.

Edith, you look lovely today!

Otto and Edith married in 1925.

The Franks had a happy family life in Frankfurt.

Anne, we need to get you some new shoes.

Can I play with my friends when I get home?

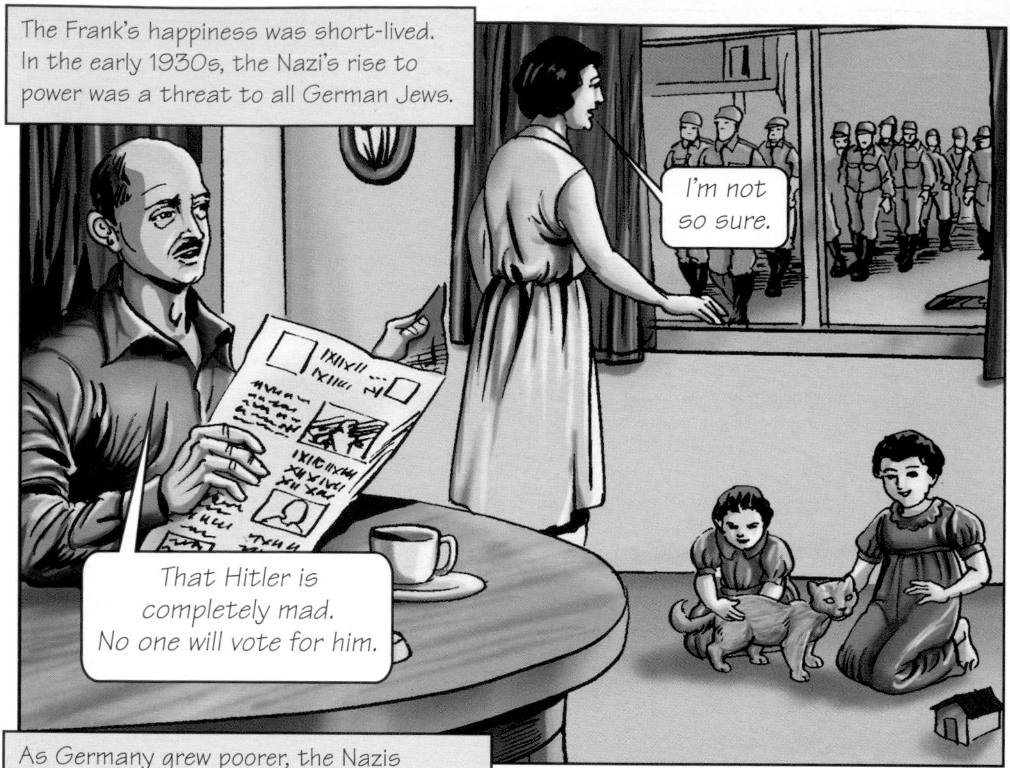

The Frank's happiness was short-lived. In the early 1930s, the Nazi's rise to power was a threat to all German Jews.
I'm not so sure.
That Hitler is completely mad. No one will vote for him.

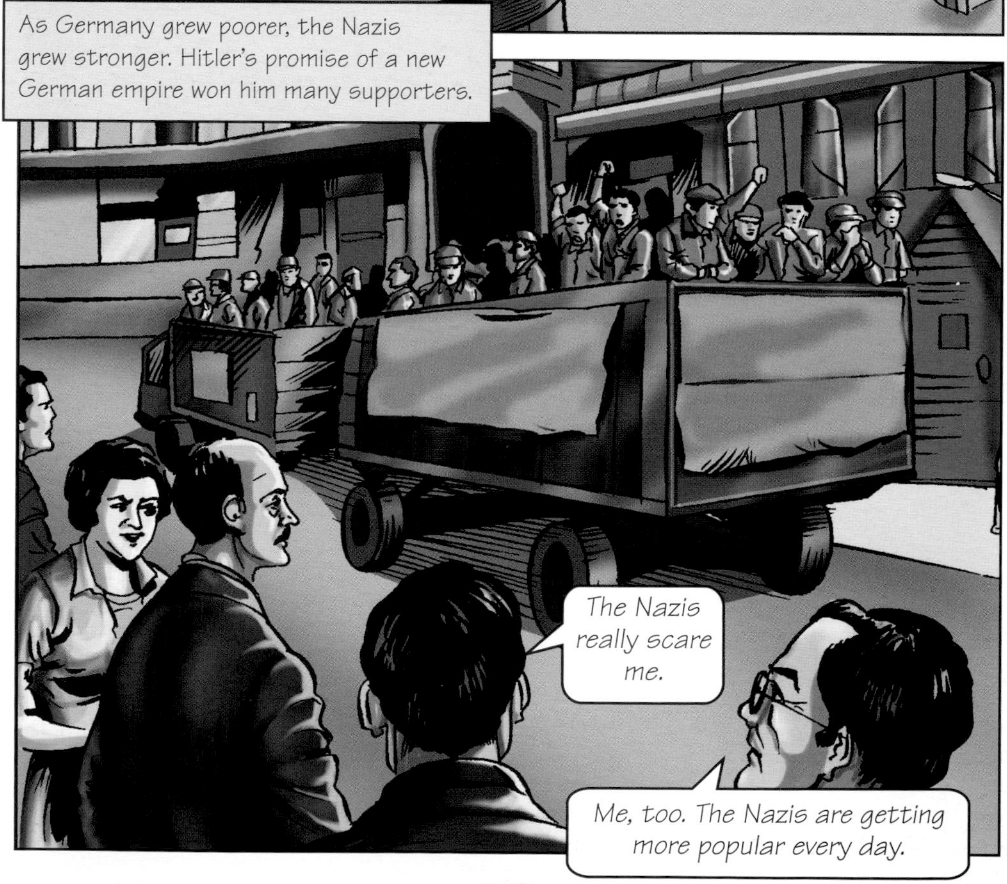

As Germany grew poorer, the Nazis grew stronger. Hitler's promise of a new German empire won him many supporters.
The Nazis really scare me.
Me, too. The Nazis are getting more popular every day.

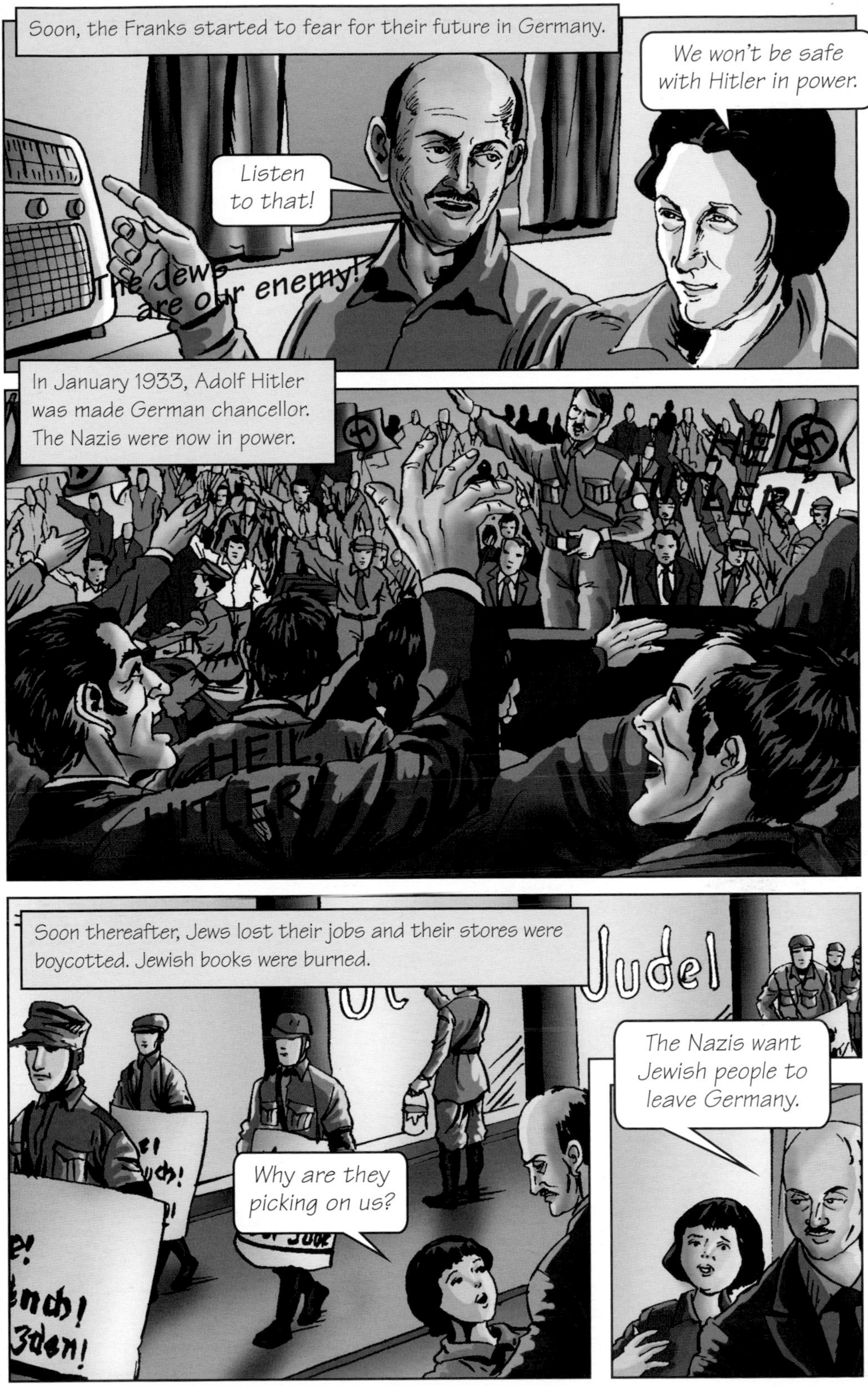

Soon, the Franks started to fear for their future in Germany.
Listen to that!
The Jews are our enemy!
We won't be safe with Hitler in power.
In January 1933, Adolf Hitler was made German chancellor. The Nazis were now in power.
HEIL, HITLER!
Soon thereafter, Jews lost their jobs and their stores were boycotted. Jewish books were burned.
Why are they picking on us?
The Nazis want Jewish people to leave Germany.

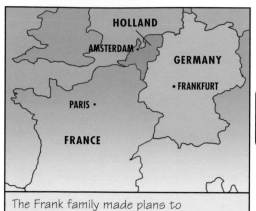

HOLLAND

AMSTERDAM

GERMANY

• FRANKFURT

PARIS •

FRANCE

The Frank family made plans to leave Germany.

The Franks decided to leave Germany.

We can be safe in Amsterdam.

In the summer of 1933, Otto Frank left for Holland.

In Amsterdam, Otto worked hard to set up a new business, the Dutch Opekta Company. He sold pectin, a powder used to make jam and gravy.

Welcome to your new home! I think you'll like it here.

Father!

Less than a year later, Edith, Margot, and Anne, who was four years old, joined Otto in Amsterdam.

Anne enjoyed her first years in Amsterdam. By the mid-1930s, the Franks had settled into a normal routine in their new apartment at 37 Merwedeplei.

Let's get Dad some flowers.

How are these?

Catch me if you can, Anne!

You're too fast, Margot!

Come and play with us, Anne!

Anne and Margot went to a Montessori school and made lots of new friends.

Say hello to Anne, everyone!

They spent their holidays at the beach.

Otto's business was doing well. In 1938, Hermann van Pels became his business partner.

It's a deal.

But the hatred the Franks had tried to leave behind followed them.

I can't believe it! How can the Nazis get away with it?

Back in Germany, many synagogues and thousands of Jewish shops had been smashed and burned by Nazi storm troopers.

Germany is for Germans, not Jews!

Smash them all!

FAST FACT

On the night of November 9, 1938, the Nazis destroyed over 7,000 Jewish shops all over Germany and attacked 267 synagogues. Because of all the broken windows, this night became known as Kristallnacht (Night of Broken Glass).

In November 1938, the Nazis began the first mass arrests of Jews, sending 30,000 men and boys to concentration camps.

Get a move on!

By 1939, half of the Jews living in Germany had fled, including Anne's uncles, who went to America.

Anne's grandmother came to live with them in Amsterdam.

Welcome to Amsterdam, Granny!

Then, in September 1939, Hitler invaded Poland. World War II had begun.

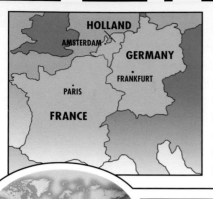

In May 1940, the Germans invaded Holland and France. The Franks were once again forced to live under Nazi rule. There was no escape—Nazi soldiers guarded the train stations and borders. Every Dutch citizen was forced to carry an identification card. This made it easy for the Germans to know who was Jewish and where they lived.

They're Nazis. They're in charge now.

Who are all those soldiers, father?

The Germans introduced ration books. Food could not be bought from a shop without them.

At first, Anne and Margot's lives didn't change much. They could still play with their friends and go to school. But everything was about to change.

The Germans, helped by Dutch Nazis, created laws against the Jews, just as they had in Germany. They forced Jews to hand over their businesses to non-Jews. Otto had expected this, and he had already signed his business over to his non-Jewish colleagues Victor Kugler and Johannes Kleiman.

I'll put the business in your names.

You can trust us. You're still the boss.

In February 1941, the Dutch Nazis raided Jewish markets. Many Jews fought back. German soldiers were called in, and over 400 Jewish men and boys were rounded up.

Did you hear about the arrests?

Nobody knows where they have been taken.

From then on, Jews in the Netherlands were in real danger.

FAST FACT The Dutch Nazis worked with the Germans. Some were paid informers who spied on Jews. The penalty for sheltering a Jew was extremely severe. Anyone providing shelter to a Jew could be taken away, shot immediately, or thrown into prison by the Nazi authorities.

Soon, Jews were not allowed in theaters, parks, or to even ride in cars and trains.

The winter of 1941 was long and hard.

Soon after Christmas, Anne's Granny became sick and died.

With all that's going on, maybe your Granny is the lucky one.

The laws became stricter. Jews now had to wear a yellow star at all times.

FAST FACT

From April 1942, Jews in Holland had to wear the yellow Star of David, bearing the word *Jood* (*Jew*) on their clothes.

Jews were not allowed outside after 8 P.M.

Don't be late!

Anne did her best to enjoy the summer. She hung out with friends, played table tennis, and ate ice-cream.

Thank you!

The Nazis are killing Jews in the camps.

We've got to go into hiding, before it's too late.

Then, the Germans began to arrest Jews just for being Jews.

Where can we hide?

There are rooms above my office.

Otto asked his partner, Mr. Van Pels, to join him.

How can we ever thank you?

There is room for both our families.

The hiding place was a secret apartment on the top two floors of Otto's office at 263 Prinsengracht.

Otto's office staff agreed to help. These friends and employees kept the business operating and risked their lives to help the Frank family survive.

Victor Kugler

Otto

Jo Kleiman

Bep Voskuijl

Miep Gies

Jan Gies

INTO HIDING

For months, the Franks and their helpers moved furniture piece by piece into the secret apartment. They stored food and supplies in the attic.

Careful with that!

Phew! These bags of flour are heavy.

The plans were going well. Then, one day, a policeman knocked on the door with a letter for Margot.

The Nazis are sending me to a work camp.

They'll kill you!

Margot was terrified.

No! They can't take you away.

There's no time to lose. We going into hiding.

They packed their bags with books and photos.

Memories mean more to me than dresses.

Otto alerted the Opekta staff.

Miep, we've got to move fast.

The next day, July 6, 1942, Anne woke up at 5.30 A.M. The Franks got ready to move.

Stuff that into my pocket.

Wear as much as you can, dear.

I feel like I'm going to the North Pole!

Margot rode ahead with Miep.

Anne walked with her parents. The Franks left notes pretending that they had left the country.

Goodbye, Moortie!

The Franks each walked with a satchel and shopping bag filled to the top.

Secret apartment

Like many houses in Amsterdam, Otto's office was next to a canal.

Anne liked the sound of the Westoren clock, which chimed every fifteen minutes.

The Franks slipped inside and went upstairs to the apartment.

Inside, Margot was waiting for the others.

I'm so glad you're safe!

Hermann

Auguste

Peter

A week later, on July 13, the van Pels family joined the Franks. Anne Frank's family and the other residents of the secret apartment were in hiding for two years. It was cramped, and they had to be very careful not to be seen or heard. For two years, they lived in fear of a knock on the door.

The secret apartment was on two floors. The Frank and Van Pels families also used the office rooms on the first floor on weekends and in the evenings.

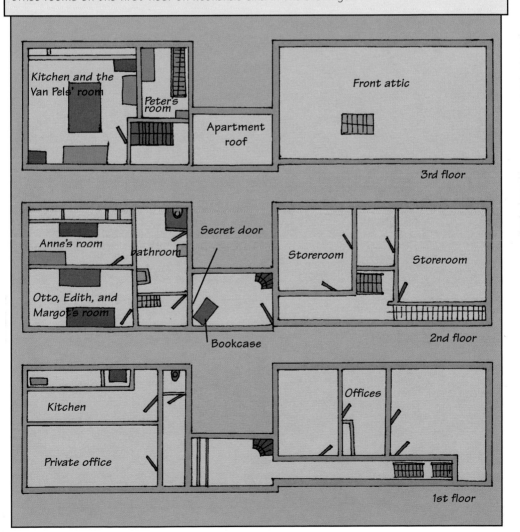

Kitchen and the Van Pels' room

Peter's room

Apartment roof

Front attic

3rd floor

Anne's room

bathroom

Secret door

Otto, Edith, and Margot's room

Bookcase

Storeroom

Storeroom

2nd floor

Kitchen

Offices

Private office

1st floor

Anne got her diary as a present on her 13th birthday, just two weeks before she went into hiding.

Anne kept a diary of her life. In the attic, she wrote about her experiences of a life in hiding.

Peter van Pels is so boring!

Anne shared her secrets with her diary.

Why does everyone always pick on me?

your DIARIES ARE IMPORTANT

I've always wanted to be a writer. I'll write my diaries like a novel.

When Anne heard on the radio that war diaries might be published, she changed the names of the people her diary. The van Pels family are called van Daan in her diary.

FAST FACT

She wrote her diary entries in the form of letters addressed to "Kitty."

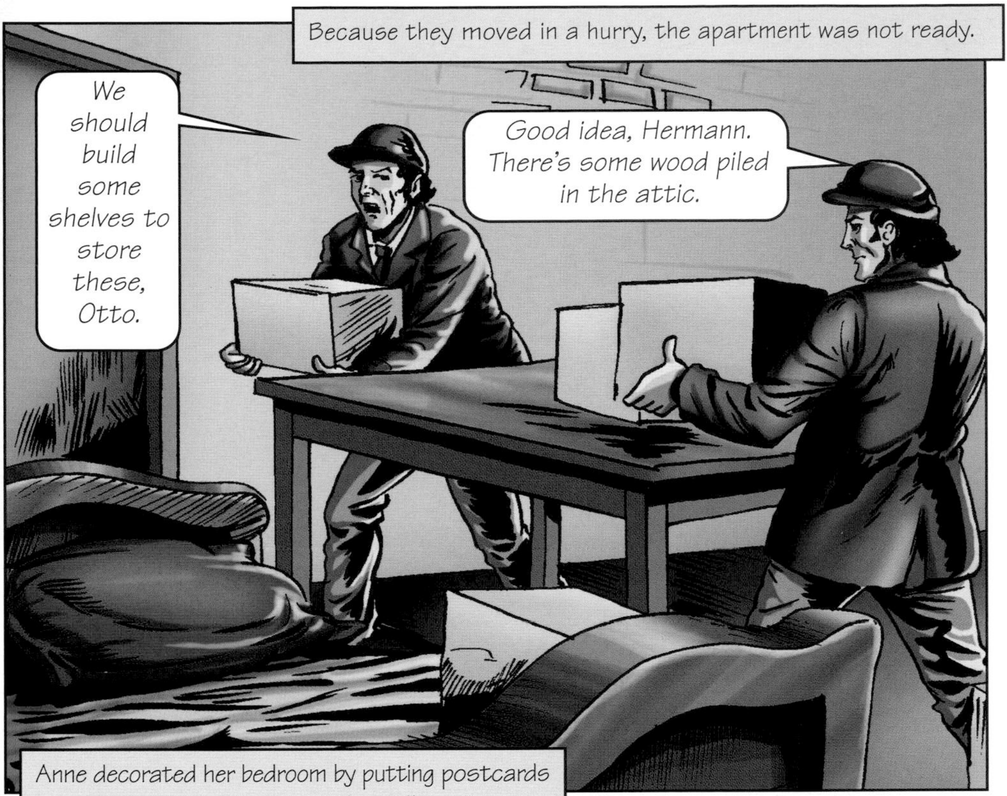
Because they moved in a hurry, the apartment was not ready.
We should build some shelves to store these, Otto.
Good idea, Hermann. There's some wood piled in the attic.

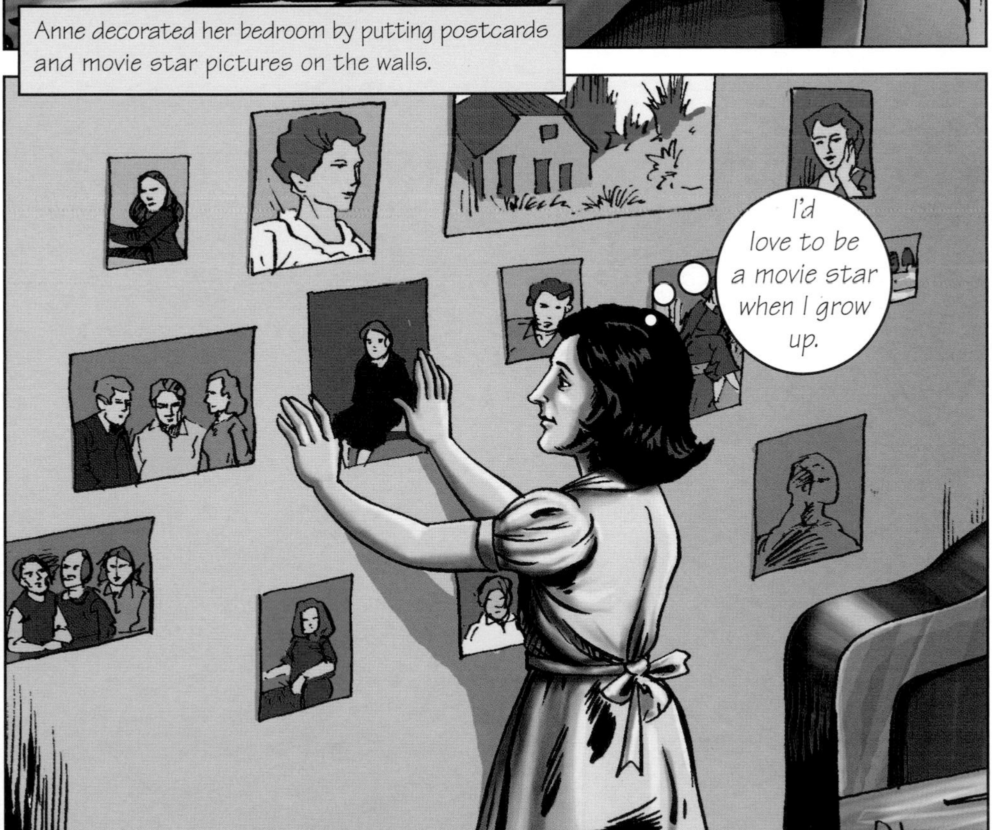
Anne decorated her bedroom by putting postcards and movie star pictures on the walls.
I'd love to be a movie star when I grow up.

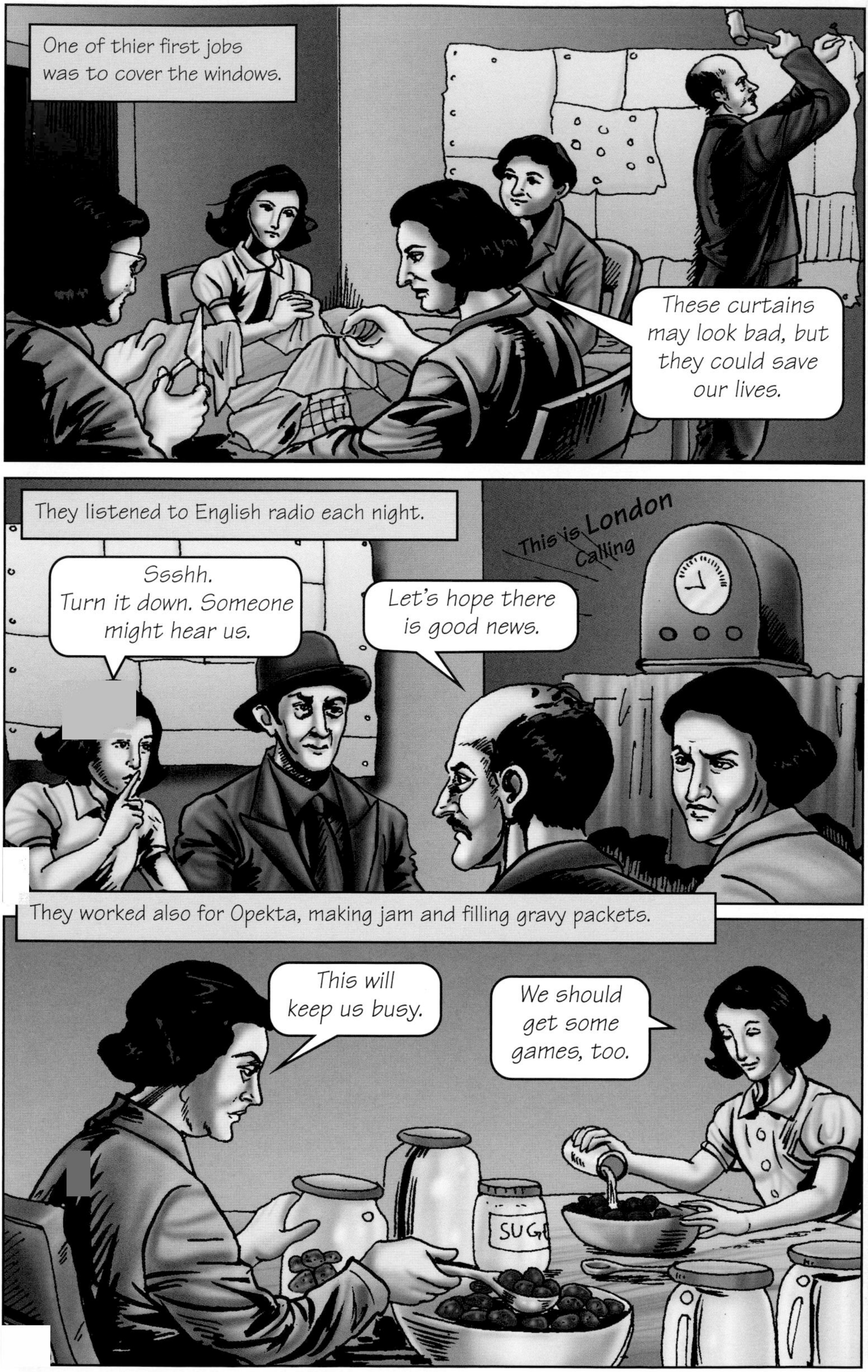
One of thier first jobs was to cover the windows.
These curtains may look bad, but they could save our lives.
They listened to English radio each night.
This is London Calling
Ssshh. Turn it down. Someone might hear us.
Let's hope there is good news.
They worked also for Opekta, making jam and filling gravy packets.
This will keep us busy.
We should get some games, too.
SUG

Mr. Kugler had a trustworthy carpenter build a bookcase in front of the entrance to the apartment.

This will open like a door. The apartment is secret now.

Miep Gies and Bep Voskuijl secretly brought food to the apartment.

Ration books could be bought illegally on the black market, but they were very expensive.

Anne found it hard being cooped up inside the apartment.

Everything has gone wrong! I should be outside, playing with my friends.

Life was either very boring or very scary!

What was that noise? It sounded like footsteps!

Anne didn't always get along with others in the apartment.

You're bossy, Mrs. van Pels!

You're just a rude little girl.

She tried to study every day, but it was hard without a teacher.

Yawn! This is so boring.

Everyone took turns to wash themselves in a tin tub.

Careful, Margot, don't let anyone see you.

Anne could never forget the danger. When a plumber came to fix the pipes, they had to be totally quiet for three days.

It's too noisy to use the toilet.

We'll have to use this pot instead.

Margot...

Sssh! If you have to speak, whisper!

At night, the girls stretched to keep themselves in shape.

Ice skates! Just what I wanted!

To pass the time, Anne imagined shopping in Switzerland with her cousin, Bernd.

A NEW OCCUPANT

On November 16, 1942, Fritz Pfeffer joined the Franks and van Pels in hiding. He was the eighth person to live in the secret apartment.

Everyone thought you had escaped to Belgium.

Join us, and have something to eat.

Mr. Pfeffer explained how their Jewish friends had been taken away by the Gestapo.

No one is spared. The sick, young, and elderly are all marched to their death.

The Gestapo were the Nazi secret police. They patrolled the streets at night looking for Jews and offered bribes to anyone who had information about them.

At times, being trapped in the apartment was a nightmare. Amsterdam was bombed by Allied planes. Anti-aircraft guns kept them awake all night. Then, Peter found rats in the attic.

But there were also good days. The Opekta staff gave everyone a gift on St. Nicholas' Day, December 5th.

Mr. Pfeffer, a dentist, pulled out two of Mrs. van Pels' teeth, much to everyone's amazement!

33

Meanwhile, as the months passed, Anne grew closer and closer to Peter van Pels.

It really helps to talk to you.

It helps me, too. I used to think you were so shy!

I think I'm falling in love. What would it be like to kiss him?

They found it hard to spend time alone.

I wish we could talk, but everyone is watching.

Finally, they kissed!

But Otto did not approve.

Be careful, Anne. Don't take it too seriously!

The Franks had been in hiding for 18 months, but now there was real hope. The Nazis were in retreat everywhere.

By the beginning of 1944, all anyone could think about was an Allied invasion and freedom!

Do you think we could be free soon?

We have to be patient.

Life was getting tougher by the day. The apartment was short on supplies.

You know that's all we have left.

Yuck! I'm sick of spinach and potatoes.

Burglars broke into the office storerooms, hoping to find food and supplies.

I hope it's not the Gestapo.

Then, one night...

CRASH!

Quick, I heard a noise downstairs!

Be careful, we don't know who it is.

Burglars had broken in to the storeroom, but Mr. van Pels scared them off.

HALT! Police!

A few minutes later, a bright light shone into the room. Was it the Gestapo? Everyone rushed back upstairs.

RUN!

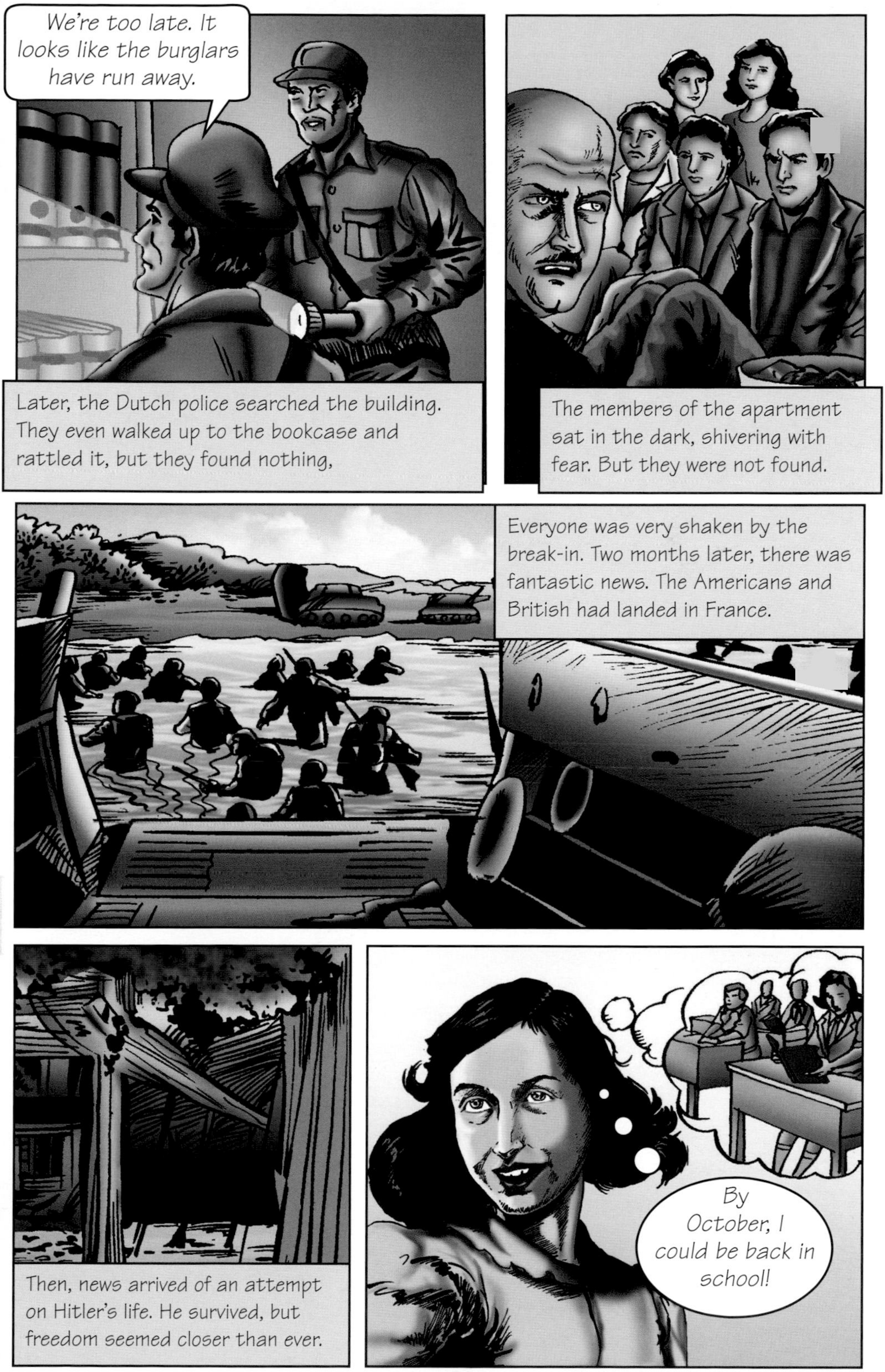
We're too late. It looks like the burglars have run away.
Later, the Dutch police searched the building. They even walked up to the bookcase and rattled it, but they found nothing,
The members of the apartment sat in the dark, shivering with fear. But they were not found.
Everyone was very shaken by the break-in. Two months later, there was fantastic news. The Americans and British had landed in France.
Then, news arrived of an attempt on Hitler's life. He survived, but freedom seemed closer than ever.
By October, I could be back in school!

Then, around 10 A.M., August 4, 1944, the Frank and van Pels' greatest fear came true. Victor Kugler heard a knock on the door to the office. Suddenly, a group of men led by a Nazi officer burst in.

They are hiding in an apartment upstairs! Don't let them escape!

The Nazis forced Mr. Kugler to show them the secret entrance to the apartment. The Franks and the van Pels had no time to escape. After two years in hiding, they had been caught.

Hand over your cash and valuables!

Take them away! Their vacation is over!

Anne and the other terrified members of the apartment were led down the stairs and forced into a waiting truck.

Shut up and get in!

Where are they taking us?

Victor Kugler and Jo Kleiman were also arrested by the police.

Miep was not arrested. She later found the scattered pages of Anne's diary in the apartment.

The Frank and the van Pels families were taken to the Westerbork camp in northern Netherlands. Then, on September 3, 1944, they were put on a train to the infamous Auschwitz death camp in Poland.

If we get separated, look after each other, my darlings.

The Nazis packed Jews onto trains like cattle. The journey took three days, and many people died on the way.

At the camps, Jews were divided into two groups, those who would work, and those who would die.

Hey, you! Get into this line!

As the Nazis retreated from the Russians, Margot and Anne were moved back to Germany to another camp, Bergen-Belsen.

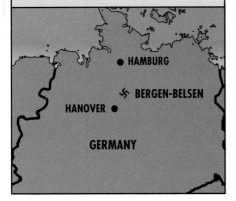

Bergen-Belsen was dirty and ridden with disease.

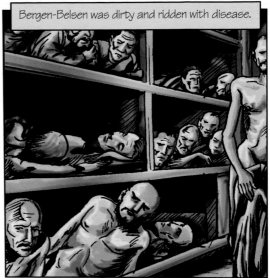

In March 1945, just weeks before their camp was freed by the British soldiers, Anne and Margot became sick with typhus. Weakened by starvation, they soon died. Anne was just 15 years old.

FAST FACT

In all, over six million Jews were murdered by the Nazis. One and a half-million victims were children. Death camps, such as Auschwitz, were giant factories of death, gassing thousands of people to death each day.

41

On May 8, 1945, the war in Europe ended. Allied troops were horrified by the terrible scenes of death, disease, and starvation they found at the camps.

Otto Frank was the only survivor of the eight who had hidden in the apartment. In 1953, he married another survivor of Auschwitz, Elfriede Markovits. Otto died in 1980, at 91.

All the Opekta helpers survived the war. Victor Kugler escaped from a Dutch prison camp, and Jo Kleiman was released because of his poor health.

Miep Gies gave Otto Anne's diary pages, which he had published in 1947. Today, over 30 million copies of Anne Frank's diary have been sold.

The house with the secret apartment at 263 Prinsengracht is now a museum.

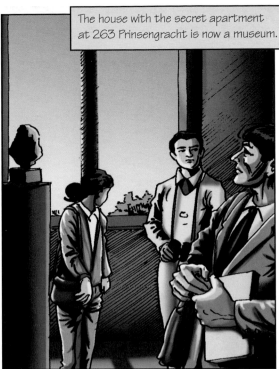

A memorial to Anne and Margot was erected at the Bergen-Belsen camp.

Anne's memory and that of all the other victims of the Nazis will live forever, thanks to her diary.

Despite being just an ordinary girl from an ordinary family, Anne Frank became one of the most famous figures of WW II thanks to her diary. Her move to Holland and into hiding typified the terror many Jews had to face on a daily basis during the Nazi rule.

1914–1918: *World War I. Otto Frank serves in the German Army.*

1925: *Otto and Edith Frank marry and settle in Frankfurt, Germany.*

June 12, 1929: *Anne Frank is born in Frankfurt, Germany.*

October 29, 1929: *The Great Depression begins, following the Wall Street stock market crash.*

Summer 1933: *Hitler becomes Chancellor of Germany and creates the first anti-Jewish laws. The Franks decide to move to the Netherlands.*

November 9–10, 1938: Kristallnacht (Night of Broken Glass). *Nazis destroy synagogues and Jewish shops across Germany.*

September 1, 1939: *World War II begins when Germany invades Poland.*

May 10, 1940: *The German army invades the Netherlands.*

June 12, 1942: *Anne receives a diary for her 13th birthday.*

July 5, 1942: *Margot is ordered to report to a labor camp. The Frank family goes into hiding the next day, joined by the van Pels family one week later. They remain in hiding for two years.*

November 16, 1942: *Fritz Pfeffer joins the Frank and van Pels families in the secret apartment.*

August 4, 1944: *The Franks are arrested, taken to a police station, then transported Westerbork, a transit camp in Holland.*

September 2, 1944: *Anne and the others in the secret apartment are sent to the Auschwitz camp.*

October 30, 1944: *Anne and her sister, Margot, are sent to the Bergen-Belsen camp.*

January 6, 1945: *Edith Frank dies of starvation at Auschwitz.*

January 7, 1945: *Auschwitz is liberated. Otto Frank is the only survivor from the secret apartment.*

March 1945: *Anne and Margot die of typhus at Bergen-Belsen.*

May 8, 1945: *Germany surrenders. World War II ends in Europe.*

Summer 1947: *Anne's diary is first published in Dutch. The first printing is 1,500 copies.*

DID YOU KNOW?

 1. When Hitler first came to power in Germany, he was very popular. He spread his ideas using radio, press, films, and by speaking at large meetings. He used his popularity to gain more and more power, banning all opposition parties and sending many opponents to concentration camps.

2. Like the Franks, thousands of Jews left Germany in large numbers from 1933 to escape life under the Nazis. But the biggest problem for them was where to go. Many countries set limits on the number of Jews they would allow to enter. Some countries even closed their borders and sent ships with Jewish refugees back to Germany.

 3. The Germans used ration cards to control the people of the Netherlands. Any Dutch person whom broke German laws lost their food. Hiding a Jew was punishable by death. One third of the Dutch people who hid Jews did not survive the war.

4. The Franks had to make a very hard decision about who to invite to live in the secret apartment. They had to rule out the Franks' best friends, the Goslars, because they were afraid their young toddler would make too much noise and give them away.

5. The Franks successfully led people to believe that they had escaped to Switzerland (a neutral country), when they were actually hiding above Otto's offices.

 6. As well as writing her diary, Anne Frank also wrote short stories, fairy tales, essays, and the beginnings of a novel during her two years in hiding. Five notebooks and more than 300 loose pages, each written by hand, survived the war, thanks to Miep Gies, who rescued them from the secret apartment.

7. When the electricity to the apartment was cut off, Anne entertained herself by watching her neighbors with a pair of binoculars through a crack in the curtains.

8. Westerbork was a camp in northeastern Netherlands, near the German border. From 1942 to 1944, the camp served as a transit camp for Jews who were being deported from the Netherlands to eastern Europe.

9. The Nazis shipped the Jews to concentration camps in rail cars, which were mainly cattle cars without windows or heating.

10. Anne Frank was one of about one million Jewish children who died during the Holocaust. Most children were sent straight to the gas chambers in concentration camps.

11. Only 4,700 of the 110,000 Jews deported from the Netherlands to the concentration camps survived. Most returning Jews had lost their families and friends. They found their houses occupied and their property stolen.

12. Anne's diary was first published in Dutch under the title Het Achterhuis, meaning The Secret Annex. So far, it has been published in 70 languages and has sold over 25 million copies.

Allies: *A group of 26 nations led by Britain, the United States, and the Soviet Union that fought against Germany, Italy, and Japan (known as the Axis) in World War II. In World War I, the Allies were a group of nations led by France, Britain, the United States, and Russia against Germany, Austria-Hungary, and Turkey.*

Auschwitz-Birkenau: *The largest Nazi concentration camp, situated in southwest Poland. Over one million Jews were murdered in this camp alone. Anne Frank and the other members of the secret apartment were sent to Auschwitz from the Westerbork camp in September 1944.*

Bergen-Belsen: *A concentration camp in northern Germany. As the Russian army advanced and Jewish camp prisoners were moved from Poland, this camp became more and more overcrowded. More than 34,000 people died in the camp from starvation and disease, including Anne and Margot.*

Black market: *The illegal selling of goods that are usually in short supply.*

Great Depression: *The Great Depression was an economic slump in North America and Europe that began in 1929 and lasted until about 1939. Millions of people around the world lost their jobs and savings.*

Concentration camps: *Prison camps that held Jews, gypsies, and political and religious opponents of the Nazis. In these labor camps, prisoners were forced to work for the Nazis. Six death camps in Poland, including Auschwitz, were built to carry out the mass murder of prisoners.*

Deportation: *Forced removal of Jews from their homes in Nazi-occupied countries. Most were transported to labor camps or death camps.*

Gestapo: *The secret police created by the Nazis to stop opposition to Hitler and the Nazi party. They were infamous for their brutal methods and were feared across occupied Europe.*

Holocaust: *The mass murder of six million European Jews by the Nazis.*

Identification card (ID card): *A card carrying information about the person who carries it, such as nationality, religion, and address. In Nazi-occupied Netherlands, ID cards had to be carried at all times. ID cards made it very easy for the Nazis to round up Jews and send them to the camps.*

Informer: *Someone who reveals confidential information, often in return for money. The Nazis relied on informers to help them hunt down Jews in hiding.*

GLOSSARY

Kristallnacht: *Meaning* The Night of Broken Glass. *On the night of November 9–10, 1938, the Nazis organized a riot against Jewish houses, synagogues, and shops in Germany and Austria. On the same night, 10,000 Jewish men and boys were arrested and sent to concentration camps.*

Jew: *Someone who practices the Jewish religion, whose mother is Jewish, or who is a member of a Jewish community. The Nazis arrested anyone with two or more Jewish grandparents or anyone married to a Jew.*

Occupation: *The control of a country by a foreign military power. Germany occupied the Netherlands and many other European countries during World War II.*

Nazi: *A shortened name for the German Workers' National Socialist party led by Adolf Hitler from 1921 to 1945.*

Rations: *A way of providing food that is in short supply. During World War II, people in many countries were given ration books that contained tokens. These tokens were given to shopkeepers to buy foods, such as meat, sugar, and eggs. Once people used their tokens, they needed another ration book to buy more food.*

Reparations: *Payment paid after the war by the losers to the winners and victims. After World War I, Germany was forced to pay reparations for the damage it had caused during the war.*

Synagogue: *A building or meeting place for Jewish worship and religious instruction.*

Storm troopers (Sturmabteilung or SA): *These ex-soldiers were used by the Nazis to threaten their political opponents. They played a important role in Adolf Hitler's rise to power in the 1930s. Storm troopers were often known as* brownshirts, *due to the color of their uniforms.*

Swastika: *An ancient religious symbol of a hooked cross that became the official symbol of the Nazi Party with its distinctive red, white, and black colors.*

Treaty of Versailles: *The peace settlement signed after World War I had ended, which blamed Germany for starting the war and forced it to pay reparations. Germany ended up paying very little of the total amount.*

Yellow star: *The six-pointed Star of David was a Jewish symbol that the Nazis forced Jews to wear to distinguish them from non-Jews. Anne Frank wore a yellow star from May 1942 until she went into hiding.*

INDEX